Heather Schow

For Adam and Rosie
D.L.

For Bryan and Sarah
P.D.

The Stopwatch
Text copyright © 1986 by David Lloyd
Illustrations copyright © 1986 by Penny Dale
First published in England by Walker Books Ltd., London
Printed in Italy. All rights reserved.
10 9 8 7 6 5 4 3 2 1
First American Edition

Library of Congress Cataloging in Publication Data
Lloyd, David, date
    The stopwatch.

    Summary: Tom times everything with his new stopwatch,
including the time it takes to retrieve the watch after
his sister borrows it.
    [1. Clocks and watches—Fiction.   2. Time—Fiction]
I. Dale, Penny, Ill.   II. Title.
PZ7.L774St 1986b   [E]   85-23847
ISBN 0-397-32193-7 (lib. bdg.)

THE STOPWATCH

BY
David Lloyd

PICTURES BY
Penny Dale

J. B. Lippincott   New York

Grandma said, "Here's a present, Tom."

It was a stopwatch.

She started it. Tom stopped it.

It took him 9 seconds.

Tom ran out of Grandma's garden.

He ran home in 3 minutes 32 seconds.

He ate a snack in 2 minutes 6 seconds.

His sister Jan said

it was too disgusting to watch.

He got undressed and into the bath and
out again in 1 minute 43 seconds.
Jan said it was cheating not to use soap.

The next morning Tom held his breath for 32 seconds.

He stood on his head for 11 seconds.

Jan said, "Let's have a staring match."

Tom lost.

He blinked after 41 seconds.

Then Tom lost his stopwatch.

He searched all over the house.

It took him a long time.

He didn't know how long because
he'd lost the stopwatch.

Jan came in.

She said, "I can ride my bike to the stor

eat a Popsicle, meet my friend,

go to the park, climb a tree,

eat another Popsicle and

ride home again in

32 minutes 58 seconds."

Tom and Jan fought like cats and dogs.

Just then Grandma arrived.

She said, "Stop that fighting!

Stop it at once!"

"Guess what, Grandma,"
Tom said.

"We just fought for exactly 7 minutes."

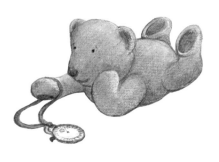